Peppa Pig™

George's Digger

Adapted by Lori C. Froeb

ISBN 978-1-5461-5344-3

10 9 8 7 6 5 4 3 2 1 25 26 27 28 29

Printed in the U.S.A. 40

Licensed by: Hasbro

First printing 2025

Book design by Sophia La Torre

SCHOLASTIC INC.

CW01582811

One sunny morning, Mummy Pig takes Peppa and George to the shops.
"Toy sale!" says Mr. Fox.

Peppa gasps. "Mummy! Can we go to the toy sale? Pleeeease!"
"Er . . . I suppose so," says Mummy Pig.

It is very busy inside Mr. Fox's shop.
"You can pick *one* thing each," says Mummy Pig,
"so choose carefully!"

George spots something special. "Dig-ga!" he says.
"Excellent choice, George!" says Mr. Fox.
"That'll be five pounds, please, Mummy Pig!"

At breakfast, Daddy Pig surprises Peppa and George. "I've been designing a new miniature golf course," he says. "Let's go see it before the grand opening later today."

George wants to stay home and play with his digger. Daddy Pig says, "You can bring your little digger, George. There'll be a real digger at the construction site, too!"

"Dig-ga!" George cheers.

At the construction site, the crew is setting up a little windmill on the course.

"DOWN! LEFT! RIGHT! NO — OTHER RIGHT!" Mr. Bull calls to the crane operator.

"Hello, Mr. Bull!" says Daddy Pig.
"I've brought Peppa and George for a tour."
"Wonderful," says Mr. Bull. "I'll show you around myself!"

First, Mr. Bull shows them the wrecking ball. "We use this to —" ***"SMASH!"*** shout Peppa and George. "Knocking things down is fun!" says Mr. Bull.

Next, Mr. Bull shows them the cement mixer. "Cement makes lovely smooth paths!"

Then, he shows them the dump truck.
"We use this for moving sand and gravel."

George isn't listening.
He has spotted something much more exciting . . .

George points. “DIG-GA!” “It looks just like yours, George!” says Peppa.

“My digger is great for digging big holes,” says Mr. Bull. “Would you like to give it a try?”

Mr. Bull drives the digger, but he lets Peppa and George press some important buttons.

"DIG! DIG!" George cheers as he helps Mr. Bull dig a ***humongous*** hole.

By the time Peppa and George's tour is complete, a crowd has gathered for the course's grand opening.

Daddy Pig cuts the ribbon with a big pair of scissors.
"I declare this miniature golf course open!"
"Hooray!" everyone cheers.

While the visitors start their games,
Mr. Bull takes Peppa, George, and
Daddy Pig to his tent for refreshments.

Everyone is enjoying a slice of delicious chocolate cake when Mr. Rhino appears. "Mr. Bull! There's a problem with the course . . ."

Oh dear!
The construction crew has forgotten something very important . . .

"There aren't any holes for the balls!" cries Peppa.

"My digger only digs very big holes. I can't fix them with it," says Mr. Bull. Luckily, George has an idea . . .

“Dig-ga!” George cheers, waving his little digger around.

Peppa whispers George’s plan to Daddy Pig and Mr. Bull, and they all squeeze into a golf cart.

Daddy Pig drives them, and George uses his little digger to dig little holes in all the right places!

Mr. Bull inspects George's work. "My digger is great for digging big holes, but George's digger is great for digging little holes!"

"I declare this miniature golf course open . . . again!" Daddy Pig tells the crowd. Everyone cheers, "Hooray!"

"Thank you for saving the day, George!" says Mr. Bull.
"Dig-ga!" George cheers.

George loves his digger.
Everyone loves George's digger!